Thanksgiving Threesome

A Super Steamy, Romantic, Erotic MMF Bisexual Threesome Between a Loving Cuckold Husband, His Hotwife, and Her Ex

Poppy Loggins

1

"And she's watching him with those eyes…" Jackie sang, snapping her head toward the driver's seat to make dramatically sexy eyes at her husband.

She shimmied. "And she's lovin' him with that body, I just know it." At the quiet, hidden upturn of Evan's lips, she added in snaps and let herself really croon.

"And he's holding her in his arms late, late at night…"

Evan bopped his head and jumped in with drumming the steering wheel before belting out the chorus with her.

Jackie grinned as he briefly took his eyes from the road to smile at her as they sang. After almost two years of marriage and now over six hours sitting beside him in stop and go traffic, she still loved every minute with him. Well, not the twenty-three minutes between realizing she *really* had to pee and finally finding the next exit, but that couldn't really be blamed on Evan.

He finished out the song, enthusiastically nailing the last guitar solo with his voice, and Jackie laughed as he started singing the next song in their playlist before it even started to play. A vibration in her lap drew her attention to her phone.

"Oh, boo!" Jackie tsked, stress heating her cheeks as she read the text from her mom. "My sister decided to come to Thanksgiving after all! Just showed up at my parents'."

"Hm, isn't that a good thing? I like Jill." Evan scanned the rear view mirror before looking to her with confusion wrinkling his brow.

"No! I mean yes! Of course. But she has the kids, and they're all going to stay at the house." Evan's grimace matched her own. Not that they weren't great kids, but they all seemed to subsist on nothing but attention, and there were four of them. She looked down at the buzz of her phone again. She rolled her eyes.

"My mom says she and Dad will take the futon because they're "not monster hosts," but there's no way I'm letting them. My dad's back is a wreck. Plus," she absently put her hand on her husband's thigh. "I've done way too many nasty things on that mattress. I don't really want to picture them there."

Evan looked at her with eyebrows high and put his free hand on top of her hand. "Nasty things?" Jackie let a smirk curl the corner of her lips and shrugged.

"Well, tempting as that is," he looked over his shoulder to change lanes. "Maybe we look for a room for rent. Or a hotel?"

"Woof, the day before Thanksgiving?" She opened the app, but wasn't feeling much hope. "Anything left will be bananas expensive," she said, and then widened her eyes at a listing. "Or straight up terrifying." She laughed and then gasped with an idea. "Ooh, maybe Gabby." She started a text.

Evan sang along with King George as Jackie waited for her friend to reply.

"Shoot," she interrupted. "She said she'd be happy to have us, but she's out of town." Her eyes widened as she read. "She's pretty sure her dog-slash-house sitter is using it as like some sort of sex weekend."

Evan quickly looked over, astonished, and the saucy little gleam in his eyes made her giggle. He nodded, lips turned down, overexaggerating reasonable agreement. "Not gonna lie, sounds like a decent Thanksgiving."

Jackie nodded and held up her phone, pretending to write out a text. "So tell her we want in?" They laughed together and she put down her phone, screwing her lips into a pout. They were about to get off on their exit.

"If we get to my parents without a plan, my mom is going to force us to stay."

Evan just gestured, helplessly pulling his mouth to the side. It's not like he knew anyone from her hometown.

An idea flipped low inside her as it rose to mind. "Grant still lives here. My ex?" She tried to project innocence as Evan glanced over. "He lives really close to my parents. With his girlfriend, I think." She looked over to him as he nodded thoughtfully, keeping his eyes glued to the road.

"Jill brought *all* the kids?"

Jackie laughed. "I'm pretty sure."

"And this would be the soccer guy or the landscaper?"

"Landscaper," she answered, imagining Grant's strong, handsome face, her fingers itching to text him.

Evan nodded slowly, scratching the stubble on his chin.

"I mean…no harm in asking, right?"

The smell of cut grass in the air when he'd get home from work.

That sunkissed and bronzed, sweaty skin.

Wide, greedy hands, confident and rough, dragging her in one effortless motion to the edge of the bed.

Jackie looked out the window and took a deep breath, hoping her husband wouldn't see the tint on her cheeks.

"Turn left," she said. They were finally in town.

Espresso and blunt smoke.

That look in his eye.

That long, thick, irresistible cock.

"Right at the light," she said. Her phone buzzed again in her lap.

She blanched and her heart bounced up into her throat. "Actually, take another left. Grant says he'll be happy to have us."

2

Evan pulled the car into a long, thin driveway, framed by lush, overflowing green and tall colors.

"Nice," he said, leaning down for a better view through the windshield. He liked the ivy cascading down the red front of the house, and the way a young yellow maple tree popped out in front.

He leaned forward for a better view of the old-looking palm trees flanking the garage.

"Isn't he our age? Landscaping must be a hell of a gig, this place and this neighborhood seem nice!"

Jackie shrugged and pulled the mirrored visor down as Evan put the car into park.

"He's lived here since junior high." She checked her teeth. "Took care of his parents through most of college, and then they left him the house."

Evan thought that sounded like the intro to a pretty sad story, but it didn't seem like his business to ask. Plus, he didn't really want to feel sorry for some poor guy he'd never even met.

Jackie's face brightened, so Evan followed her eyes toward one of the most handsome men he'd ever seen in real life. He left the front door open and strolled across his little courtyard oasis, a big, welcoming smile on his scruffy, rakish face.

"Uh," Evan started, a laugh in his voice. They unbuckled their seatbelts. "You didn't tell me he was an Abercrombie model." He thought he saw a blush rise up her cheeks.

"That was a long time ago." She grinned out the window and waved. "And never Abercrombie, just some local stuff."

Evan's jaw dropped open - he had been joking - but looking again at the tall, broad-shouldered man, he was pretty sure she was telling the truth. Suddenly more unsure than he had been before, he followed Jackie's lead and got out of the car.

"Hey, hey!" The handsome man said, meeting Jackie's wide open arms with a bear hug.

Jealousy flipped low in Evan, but he quickly pushed it down. He had never been the type of guy to be possessive of his wife, and he wasn't about to start now.

But, damn, they seemed to hold that hug a long time.

"Hey man! Grant." The man grinned and looked him in the eye while extending his hand, and Evan shrank as he shook it.

"Evan." He swallowed hard, unsure why embarrassment filled him. He forced himself to let go. He looked over to his wife, who was looking at Grant, and chilled at the gleam in her eyes.

Oh, fuck.

What did we get ourselves into?

3

"Wait, what do you mean, you're staying at Grant's?" Jill whispered vigorously as she grasped her fingertips into Jackie's arm. Jackie giggled and grabbed her back.

"Nothing!" She answered, mocking her sister's intensity in her eyes and voice. "And your tolerance has really changed since having kids!" She laughed and pointed at the still-quarter-full beer Jill had been nursing since the kids went to bed.

"No...friggin' joke," Jill agreed, pointing in Jackie's face with a snicker, and put the bottle down on the table. "But also, pssshh…" Jill sounded like a released airlock brake as she leaned back on their parents' couch. "You said you were staying with a friend." She looked her sister pointedly in the eye. "Grant's not a friend. He's your ex." She walked her fingers down Jackie's arm like little marching legs. "Your hot, sexy, hung-as-hell ex."

"Jill!"

Jill giggled, immensely pleased with herself, and Jackie joined her, looking across the long room to catch eyes with her husband. He lifted his brows in good-natured drama, as her father showed him what she was sure was his 400th picture of elk.

Jill made her fingers do the can-can along Jackie's wrist. "Eh, I think you should fuck him," she said, holding her hand out as if presenting an obvious fact.

"Oh my god, Christ, Jill!"

"Whaaat?" Jill rolled her eyes and waved her hands. "I know, I know. "I love Evan. I'm married to Evan.""

Jackie nodded her head with a look of, *yeah, exactly, Dumbass!* written clearly all over her face.

"So have him join in." Jill shrugged. "I always thought he was gay, anyway."

"Jill!" Jackie repeated for what felt like the dozenth time, and covered her red, giggling face with her hands. "I don't even want to fuck Grant," she said, though a wave of guilt rose up as she did. "Plus, I think he lives with his girlfriend. And my husband isn't gay." She looked at her sister seriously and raised her eyebrows as if uniquely impressed. "The man *eats. Puss.*"

The sisters peeled into giggles.

Despite the wrench she threw into plans, Jackie was thankful her sister was there. She leaned her head on Jill's shoulder and smiled over at Evan, trying to ignore the nagging guilt rumbling inside.

She couldn't wait to get back to Grant's.

4

Evan and Jackie snuck into Grant's house, unsure of he'd already be sleeping. Instead, they found the kitchen light on, with a shirtless Grant at the stove.

Somehow angry at the sight of his abs, Evan excused himself to change in the guest room; his good impression sweater was itchy.

In the dark quiet, he noticed his heart beating too fast, and changing into gym shorts gave some idea where the blood might be flowing.

The desire to get himself back between Jackie and her ex was rivaled only by the craving set off by the smell of crisp bacon. Both sent him hurrying back to the kitchen, but he stopped in his tracks before he even walked in.

Jackie rested her hip on the kitchen island, and Grant stepped too close, leaning into her space. Evan couldn't miss the slight arch of her back.

Just as indignation was rising inside Evan (which was honestly not the only thing rising up), Grant reached and grabbed a large bottle that had been blocked by Jackie's back.

"Whiskey?" He asked, turning from her with a grin and grabbing three glasses. Jackie nodded, a sly smile across her face.

"Yes, please."

"Straight up?"

Jackie didn't answer, but her smile grew, and Grant reached in the freezer for ice.

"Yeah," he said, easy arrogance deepening a smile line on his face. He jiggled the shaker. "I know how you like it."

Evan's stomach dropped as he stood watching, filling with anger, betrayal, and something else he didn't have the wherewithal to name.

Grant handed the glass to Jackie, then glanced toward the door frame. His eyes crinkled as they met Evan's, and he raised up the shaker in welcome. "Oh, hey man!" He didn't look the least bit ashamed. "Whiskey?"

Evan nodded and finally entered the room. "Thanks." He told himself to calm down, and took a sip of the spirit. He welcomed the burn.

After less than half a glass, all of Evan's anger had faded, but the something unnameable grew.

Grant set a plate of popping bacon on the table. "I know Jackie likes it basically raw," Jackie stuck out a goofily defiant tongue as she reached for a floppy strip, and Grant grinned at her before turning his charm on Evan. "But there'll be better stuff in a second if you like it more firm, like me."

Evan chuckled, but more out of nerves than humor. "I'm with you," he said with a finger-gun, and then promptly filled with embarrassment. He was a people-pleaser anyway, but *man,* he wanted this guy to like him.

Grant turned back with a plate of crisped bacon, pointing his chin out to welcome Evan to it. He noticed the light bounce off a few grease spots that had splattered Grant's abs, but quickly looked away when he felt his eyes on him.

"Mm," Evan appreciated, as the meat practically melted on his tongue. "You always make night-bacon?" He asked, holding it up between bites. It was almost eleven.

"Nah," Grant answered, pecs flexing as he tipped his cast iron over an old can to collect the grease. Why couldn't Evan stop looking at him? "Usually an early bird, just getting a jump on the side

I'm taking to my uncle's tomorrow. Wasn't sure if you two will need the kitchen." Jackie and Evan widened their eyes at each other, realizing they should probably figure out something to take.

"Besides, I remembered how much this one likes her late-night meat."

The comment was annoying to Evan, but he told himself to overlook it. He was probably the only one with the pervy mind of a teen. After all, whenever Jackie stayed awake late, her go-to snack really was leftover chicken or cold-cuts. Maybe it was the truth of his statement that was actually annoying.

Jackie made a face at Evan. "We should probably figure out something to take to my parents," she said, but then dismissively waved her hand and took another sip of her whiskey. "Eh, I'll ask my mom in the morning."

"Well, if you need the kitchen tomorrow, feel free to hop in. I'm a good boy, I know how to share."

Jackie threw her arms around Evan as soon as the guest door closed. She pressed her lips to his, an intoxicating blend of toothpaste and whiskey, and his heartbeat immediately responded.

A slightly-buzzed flurry of hands and peeled off clothes, the couple stumbled back toward the bed. With a grin, Jackie pushed him, and he "oomph"ed as he fell onto the bed. God, Jackie was sexy, standing before him in nothing but fuck-me-eyes and a smile.

Evan's cock was now fully erect (or maybe it already was), and, a bit dizzy with the the whir of arousal, he could only lie there and stare at her tits.

She seemed to enjoy the spell she'd cast on him, and slowly, taunting, pulled the waves of her mane up off her neck. He watched her slithering fingertips descend over her torso, and parched as she dipped down below. Her eyes glittered as she grinned open-mouthed at him, seeming to enjoy the way he watched her almost as much as her touch.

She walked to the edge of the bed, still touching herself, holding Evan's eyes and taking his breath. With a gasp, she pulled her hand from between her legs and reached out to Evan's throbbing hard cock.

"I'm so wet," she whispered, and put her silky, slick fingers gently on the head.

"Oh my god," Evan whispered, her touch tightening him to the core.

You know why she's already so wet, don't you?

"You like that?" She asked glibly, barely stroking his shaft, and all he could do was nod.

"You like that I'm already so wet?"

Yes, he thought desperately. *Yes, yes, yes.*

So wet I can already hop on and just…" she abandoned his cock and quickly climbed on the bed, dripping on his leg as she moved up to straddle him.

"Oh, Jackie, fuck!" He grunted as she mounted him, the tip of his cock sinking immediately into her body. She lifted herself almost all the way off, then sat down and took him all the way in. He moaned and grabbed her hips, overtaken by the instinct to plow deep inside. He loved the wicked look in her eye.

I wonder if Grant is bigger than me.

The intrusive thought was a shock to his balls, and he bucked wildly under his wife.

He had thought a few times that night - was staying with Jackie's ex a good idea, or foolishly asking for trouble? However, he didn't imagine another way this night would have ended with whiskey, bacon, and hot cowgirl sex, so for now, he was happy they came.

5

Awoken by the smell of espresso and the crisp autumn breeze from the window, Jackie looked over to see her husband still heavy with sleep. She smiled, remembering his burst of urgent energy the night before.

After padding into the kitchen alone, Jackie opened a drawer to find everything needed to make herself an espresso and smiled - still the same as when she set it up years ago.

Hot mug in hand and grabbing a blanket off the back of the couch, Jackie let herself out the back sliding glass door into Grant's cute little deck. A pile of cushions sat piled under the eaves to avoid morning dew, and some of the old faded patterns brought a swell of sweet memories.

A skunky wisp of air snapped her out of her thoughts, pulling her attention to the old gazebo Grant had salvaged and put up under a shroud of big, droopy trees.

She leaned on the chipped white wood rails and kept her voice soft as to not startle him. "Still doing that?"

He smiled up broadly at her and pulled the small, handrolled joint from his mouth. The dry paper tugged at his lip, reminding Jackie of hot, nipping teeth. She was suddenly aware of her wild hair, and tucked a corner behind her ear.

"Maybe," he answered with an easy grin, and made an inviting motion. "Still joining in?"

Jackie grinned and moved through the entrance, joining him down on the floor. Holding the blanket together around her shoulders with one hand, she accepted the joint from Grant and took two light puffs. She looked over at him through one open eye while she happily held in her breath. Grant smiled at her as she slowly exhaled, and took another drag himself.

"I always loved it back here," Jackie said wistfully, turning her attention to the trees. Light, misty fog seemed to cling to their branches.

"Still my favorite place," he said, contented, and leaned his head back against a rail.

"I thought that was Warner's Cove," she said teasingly, eyes dancing with lurid memory as she grinned around the filter in her mouth.

Grant tilted his chin up with a satisfied smirk and looked off into the trees. "Yeah," he said, nodding while inhaling slowly, then looked at her playfully in the eyes. "Depends who I'm with."

Jackie blushed, and the stir between her legs told her she needed to think of other things.

"Is your girlfriend doing Thanksgiving with her family this year?" She realized she hadn't seen her yet.

"Nah, we broke up months ago."

Duh. Jackie hadn't seen any pictures of them or girly stuff.

"Oh no!" She said, ashamed at the small part of herself that was pleased. "What happened?"

He shrugged and passed her the joint as he held in his breath. "Ah, it's alright. We weren't meant to be." He exhaled slowly and rounded it out with a low laugh. "She walked in on me watching gay porn." He relit the tip, then passed it back over to Jackie and looked at her, amusement bright in his face. "She did not like that."

Jackie tried and failed to keep her eyeballs in check, as they expanded along with her lungs. She coughed, sputtering a laugh of smoke and surprise.

"You're gay?" She didn't intend to sound so incredulous, but, well, her previous experiences with him had strongky - *firmly* - indicated othersmwise.

Grant laughed, then let his eyes linger over her lips. She heated.

"What do you think?"

Jackie blushed and looked out to the trees, trying to bite back a smile.

Grant chuckled again. "Bi. Pan." He ashed and relit the joint with a confident shrug. "I don't know. I want what I want." His eyes dropped again to her mouth, and she didn't exactly discourage him with the way she put the joint to her lips.

"Well, I hope you get it," she said, drawing in smoke. "I hope you get whatever you want."

6

A shadow passed over his face, and the smell of his very first concert as a teen drifted into his subconscious. A short guitar riff from one of songs set the for-some-reason quickening pace of his heart. Without even opening eyes, he knew he was out of place. Was he upside down in his bed?

No, he was somewhere else.

In someone else's bed.

A shadow.

His heartbeat.

A sudden rush of wet heat slipping over his cock.

"Oh god." The words were a whisper, escaping before he could even open his eyes.

His wife knelt beside him on the bed, messy hair, in his hoodie, and eyes already bright as the morning. She grinned as she licked circles around his head.

"Good morning," she said cheerfully, and then swallowed his shaft. All Evan could do was groan.

"Fu..." he exhaled, eyes closed, and his hand snaked into her hair. "What...what?"

Jackie popped off of his tip with a grin. "I'm waking you up with a blowjob." She slid him back over her tongue.

He relaxed and savored every stroke of her tongue. She was getting sloppy, and it felt like heaven.

"Do you smell like weed?"

"Mmhmm," she confirmed, slurping his shaft, and looking right into his still-drowsy eyes as she took him right down to his balls.

She gasped as she came off, and replaced her mouth with her hand. "I couldn't sleep, and when Grant offered, I couldn't resist." Her words sent a clench through his balls, and she slobbered again on his head.

"He invited you out to share." She alternated giving pleasure with her mouth and her hands, but her voice and eye contact were really what had him so hard.

"So here's my plan-"

Evan struggled to listen as his breathing shallowed and quickened in pace.

"You'll go share me with Grant-"

"What?" Electricity zinged down his shaft

"You and me will go share with Grant-"

Oh.

Why had he been so excited?

"Then we can just walk to brunch at my parents."

"Uh huh."

"Then we'll come back here. Do a little cooking…"

How did she make a list sound seductive?

"And then? If there's time?" She looked him right in the eyes and deepened her suck, before sliding off and wiping her lip with a mischievous smirk. "Maybe I'll finish you off."

"What?" He gasped as Jackie stood up, leaving him red, hard, and throbbing in the air. "Oh, no!" He groaned with a laugh, and covered his face with his hands. He could die from frustration, but damn, what a hot way to go.

"So rude!" He exclaimed, peering down to his cock, tingling with the confusing rush that came from denial. "What am I supposed to do with this?"

She shrugged, delight shining clear in her eyes. "Take it with you."

7

Jackie held Evan's eye as she squirted whipped cream on her waffle, aiming for absurdly sexual. His nostrils flared as he held back a laugh, so she grinned, knowing she had nailed it. This trip was turning out even more fun than she had imagined.

As Jackie lingered over fruit salad, Evan and her dad rounded up the kids for their first foam football game of the day.

"So how's it going staying with Grant?" Jill asked, as soon as their mom left the table. Jackie stabbed a blueberry and grinned.

"Fine," she said, popping it happily between her teeth. "Fun."

Jill's eyes glittered. "Fuck him yet?" She whispered playfully.

"No," Jackie started, glancing out the window, doing a mental count of kids to make sure none would appear right behind her. "But I do really want to." She grimaced, then rolled her eyes and the smugness of her sisters face. She put on an overly goofy voice. "You were right."

She paused and listened, making sure her mom was still gone. She continued in a whisper anyway. "He's single now. And so sexy. No, Jill." She interrupted her sister's nodding, telegraphing sincerity hard with her eyes. "Like, even more than when I dated him." Jill's eyes widened a bit. "He's, like, thicker. More solid. Like he's been lifting weights. And he keeps a little scruff now." She motioned to her own face, which was getting a little red. She looked around to confirm privacy again.

"And he said he's bi or pan, quote, "I want what I want."" She started to hiss at her sister. "And ever since you said you always thought Evan was gay, I can't stop thinking about the two of them fucking!" She groaned and put her hands to her forehead, pushing back the waves of her hair.

Jill seemed simply tickled. She laughed. "K, that's hot."

Jackie laughed along and shouted. "I know!"

Jill's second oldest child came bursting through the back door needing help with an owie. Jackie met eyes with her husband through the big picture window and he guiltily bared his teeth with an "oops." He pointed to himself, then mimed out pushing a child, and shrugged with his hands out, like, "what can you do?" Jackie laughed at the insinuation, having already heard the real cause from her nephew, and knowing Evan would never even harm a housebug. Plus, he believed having fun was more important than winning (always, but especially when versus a child.)

She watched as her husband theatrically Heismaned through the children, letting them believe they were slowing him down. With grand gestures, he "stumbled," allowing the kids to tackle him down. Football forgotten, they continued to tackle her laughing husband, till he waved his arms in surrender.

He said something to the kids and they gathered at his arms, picking up his hands and bracing, as if about to pull him up onto his feet. Even unable to hear, she could see the big buildup as Evan counted to three.

At once, all kids lifted and hoisted and yanked - but Evan didn't help them, so his body just didn't budge. Jackie's father roared with laughter as he watched from under a tree.

All other thoughts cleared away for the moment as she watched her husband be silly and fun in the yard. She loved him. She wanted him.

She was so thankful to be his.

8

Evan stood alone in Grant's kitchen, looking for a cutting board and sharp knife.

It felt a bit awkward to be in a near-stranger's kitchen, but he had agreed to do the mise en place while Jackie went to the store for things to make sides.

Evan offered to do the shopping, but Jackie had lovingly patted his chest. "Do you know where the store is?" She'd teased, then gave him a know-it-all face. "And you think I want to cut up all those onions??"

The stinging started gently, but as he continued to cut, the onions exponentially burned in his eyes.

Grant came through his front door in a tight, sweaty t-shirt with a spattering of dirt, and Evan looked up at him with tears in his eyes.

"Hey, man," Grant paused when he saw him, concern and suspicion wrinkling his brow. "You ok?"

"Yeah," Evan laughed, sniffling, and wiped his tears with the back of his hand. He brandished the knife as explanation. "Thanks for the onions. Whew!"

He shook his head, a bit embarrassed, and sniffed to try to clear the sting from his sinuses.

Grant laughed, left his muddy shoes by the door, and sauntered into the kitchen. Evan felt his eyes on him and coached himself to stay focused on his cuts.

"You a chef, Evan? Or just really good with your hands?"

He blushed. "I, uh," he cleared his throat of nerves and looked away as he washed up. "Not a chef." There was no way he could get himself to say he was "good with his hands." It felt dangerous.

Grant laughed and moved to use the sink before Evan was fully out of the way, and the gentle bump of his shoulder felt like a sack of rocks being dropped on his balls. The smell of sweat hit his nose in a way that made him feel more like a man.

"Ever been up to the cliffs?" Grant asked, pointing vaguely into the air with his soapy hands.

"No, I've only come to town twice, and Jackie's family aren't big hikers."

"Oh yeah," Grant breathed out a laugh, nodding. He looked him in the eye, confidently amused. "Bet they took you wine tasting at least once, though."

Evan laughed. It was disconcerting to be known by this man only because of how well he had known his wife, but was also strangely comforting and pleasant. He wanted Grant to know him.

"Well, if you wanna go on a hike while you're here, let me know." He grinned at him as he dried his hands. "I'd be happy to take you." He hung the dish towel over its hook and looked back at Evan. "Anytime."

Evan hated the easiness with which he blushed around Grant. It made him feel tiny and weak, inexperienced, and confused.

He didn't want it to stop.

The front door opened and Jackie walked in with a big paper bag in her hands. Evan's heart pounded in his throat; he felt guilty, but didn't know why.

"Jackie!" Grant called out. His smile lit the room.

"Hey, Babe!" Evan added, and kissed her as she came into the kitchen. He lips were spice on his, and, despite the chasteness, felt himself heat and pinken knowing Grant was watching.

"Okay," Jackie started unloading the bag. "Corn casserole and scalloped potatoes with caramelized onions." Both the men made appreciative sounds of hunger. Jackie looked over hopefully to Grant. "You're sure it's ok to tie up the oven and a burner or two?"

"Yep, I only need one burner. Help yourself to the rest." He grinned and wiggled his eyebrows at Evan as Jackie knelt down to pull out a pan. "Might get a little hot in here."

9

Jackie leaned back into her chair, contented, and tried to be sly as she undid the button of her pants. It was the point of Thanksgiving where nearly everybody complained, "Oh, I should have had one less bite of..." and then absently ate another forkful of pie.

Her phone buzzed. "Ummm, are you undressing at family dinner?"

She snapped her attention up to find Evan already staring at her, smiling, his phone in his hands. She texted back as her mom detailed all the people she had run into at the store.

"Sorry, yes, I'm REALLY HORNY," she wrote, adding in a couple eggplants and a peach for good measure. She sent it and immediately typed up another. "Is this...not....is this not a good time???"

She looked up to see his shoulders shaking, and made a goofy little face when he looked up.

"TWO eggplants?" His new text read. "Someone is greedy. Or hungry?"

Both, she thought, even though Thanksgiving had overly satiated her stomach. She put down her phone and just winked at him, too swirling-full of thoughts to trust herself not to say something foolish.

The sight of Evan standing chest to chest with Grant, the larger man leaning too far into his space, a look of hot confusion burning in her husband's eyes, still thrived inside Jackie's memory. And between her legs.

She took a sip of her drink.

"Are we gonna meet Grant's girlfriend?" Evan had asked as they changed clothes before leaving for dinner. "He never really talks about her."

"Oh," Jackie winced. "I didn't know before, but I guess they broke up."

"Oh." His eyes seemed nervous. Jackie wasn't sure what to say.

"Well, a guy like that? Single?" Evan pulled on a sweater and shook his head with a laugh. "He must be pulling in the ladies left and right!"

Jackie nodded and chuckled too, eyeing him in the mirror as she fixed her hair. "Guys, too."

Evan paused and snapped his eyes to her in the mirror. "What? He's gay?"

She flushed, but tried to seem nonchalant. "No. Guys and girls. As he put it, he wants what he wants."

"Hmm. Bet he gets what he wants, too."

Jackie held his reflection's gaze before blushing and looking back to herself with a smile. "Probably."

Jackie and Jill had offered to take care of the dishes - Jill washing, Jackie drying, just like in the old days. Evan had offered to help, but some of the kids had convinced him they needed an even number of board game competitors, and stole him away for their team.

"You seem so happy with him," Jill smiled as she passed her a pan.

Jackie nodded without hesitation. "Ugh, I am, it's disgusting." She teasingly rolled her eyes at herself and Jill laughed.

"Revolting!" She said, passing off another pan. "No, it's cute. Even if you were, like, spraying pheromones all over Thanksgiving dinner."

Jackie snapped her with the dish towel, but couldn't help but giggle. "Gross, Jill!"

Jill grinned. "Sorry." But she certainly wasn't. She had always loved needling her sister. "And sorry for..." she looked surreptitiously around the kitchen, and out through the entry, lowering her voice even though no one was nearby.

"...the shit I was saying last night." She giggled again, but then looked at Jackie sincerely. "I really love Evan, he's the best. I wasn't trying to tell you to cheat on him."

Jackie bit back a smile and raised her eyebrow in accusation.

"Okay, okay, I was." She laughed again. "But I didn't mean it. And I don't think you should." She went back to scrubbing dishes as if she'd moved on from her thought, but Jackie knew her well enough to know more was coming. She just leaned on the counter, staring at her in amusement till she bubbled over snickering again.

"I just think anyone who has the opportunity to get it put in by that man should." Jackie made a face at the phrase, which just seemed to make Jill feel more sure. "Anyone who doesn't is a fool." She shrugged.

Jackie felt a blush pinch her cheeks and continued drying an already dried bowl. "I actually think I agree with you there." Her heart pounded high in her throat.

Jill looked over with curious eyes as she felt around in search of the drain plug and pulled.

Graphic, lewd thoughts of being in bed with both Evan and Grant had been threatening to surface all day, but Jackie shook them off and put herself back in the silly as she dried her hands and pointed sharply at her sister.

"Maybe *you* should go see if you can "get it put in," you horndog."

Jill feigned offense, pulling her head back and raising her still-soapy hand to her chest. "Wow. How dare you. I'm a married mother of four, Jackie." She shook her head in mock disgust, grabbed the towel, and tsked. "Crass and vulgar."

The sisters held eyes for a moment, bright and shining, then dissolved into giggles again.

10

Jackie's parents had served champagne (or "bubbly," as her dad kept saying, refusing to use the technically-incorrect term) after the kids went to bed, and Evan was grateful Grant lived so close he and Jackie could just walk back.

They held hands as they walked through the night, and Jackie leaned into him, clearly seeking the heat of his body against the cool, damp air. He put his arm around her as they walked in step.

"Brr!" She chattered, smiling up at him sweetly, nose and cheeks bright pink like a cartoon. He paused his feet and drew her into him, grinning broadly as she squealed. He wrapped his arms around her, enveloping her in his coat, and leaned down to give her a kiss.

Her nose was freezing as it bumped on his cheek, but he still felt warmed as she hungrily leaned into his lips. She slid her hands up over his chest and grabbed his sweater, opening her mouth for his tongue.

Warm and needy, his tongue prodded hers, and he chilled as her hands snaked up his neck. Hot blood flowed between them, causing a bounce in the front of his pants.

Suddenly remembering they were out on the sidewalk, Evan broke apart from their kiss. "We gotta get back," he breathed, and she looked at him with a devilish smirk. She rolled her body against him before turning and grabbing his hand.

"What happens when we get back?" She looked up at him with seduction in her eyes. The champagne bubbles fluttered happily through his mind.

"I fuck you, Baby."

Jackie grinned, clearly satisfied with his answer, and liked him faster toward the house. She looked at him with an expressive pout.

"What if Grant's home?"

"Then maybe we both…" the mix of his rising cock and champagne swimminess got the better of him, but he caught himself before he completed his thought. "Uh, maybe we both just be quiet then." The way she looked at him, he thought she probably knew what he had wanted to say.

"Mmhmm," she agreed, tempting Evan with the fire in her eyes, and the naughty upturned corner of her lips.

He excitedly picked up his pace as he followed his wife up the driveway, and entered Grant's code to the garage. Hands on her hips, Evan leaned her against the wall and kissed her as they waited for the garage door to rise.

Giggling, she tugged his hand forward, and together they stumbled, still kissing as they made their way into the house.

"I don't think he's home yet," Evan panted as he peeled off Jackie's coat as they kissed.

"I don't think so," Jackie said, urgently trying to rid Evan of his jacket, until he let go of her and just helped her along. She turned her head to the side with a gasp as he forcefully returned his lips to her neck. "I don't smell him here," she murmured.

The words, along with the tone of her voice, rushed hot jealousy through to the tip of his dick, lengthening him on the way. He knew the smell she meant. She reached for his zipper and he turned, pressing her into the wall next to Grant's open bedroom door. The room was dark and empty.

"Do you wish he was? Here?" Evan rasped, sliding his hand up her shirt and enjoying the way her nails dug into his neck.

Jackie gave up on his zipper and stroked him through his pants. "Kind of."

Evan pinned her to the wall with his hips and kissed her hard.

Why was that the answer you wanted? He tingled and buzzed, and let them but of extra freedom from champagne carry him away.

"You wanted to come in and find him shirtless again?"

Jackie gasped and yanked on his zipper again, trying desperately to get into his pants. "Yes," she breathed, and to Evan it sounded like a plea.

He kneaded her breast underneath her sweater and they fumbled toward the guest room, a flurry of hands and tongues and moans.

"Wanted him to back you up against the counter again?"

"Oh, yeah."

He hadn't been able to get the image out of his mind. He liked it.

"Wanted him to lift you up and grab onto your thighs?" He roughly slid a hand under her thigh and she groaned as she lifted it up, rocking her hips into his body. "Pull you to him?"

"God, Evan!" She pushed off the door frame against him, thrusting them into the room. "Yes!"

He pushed her onto the bed and, in a rush, opened his pants and pulled out his hard, solid cock. He grabbed himself while looking down at his wife, kicking her pants off her legs.

"Tell me about him," he said, climbing on top of his wife. He didn't know what had come over him, but it wasn't just the champagne. He had been having increasing thoughts and questions about Grant, and he no longer could hold them back. He slid his tip through her slick, wet folds and looked her close in the eye.

"Tell me about his cock."

11

Jackie couldn't believe her ears, especially now that they thundered with the frantic beat of her heart. However, even if her ears weren't to be trusted, the heat in his eyes was unmistakable. She dripped around her husband's tip, wondering how much he could bear, and if he *actually* wanted to hear the truth.

"Oh, are you sure, Baby?" She rocked under him, sliding her clit against his shaft.

He nodded and slipped quickly inside her. "Yeah." He pulled out and slid over her clit again. "Tell me."

Jackie closed her eyes and let pleasure take over her face as she let in the detailed memories she'd been trying not to dwell on.

"Oh, god, Baby, he's so big." She gasped as Evan thrust hard inside her.

"Yeah?" He grunted, and she bit her lip.

"Oh yeah." He looked at her, hungry for more. "He's thick. Really thick." She closed her eyes again as her husband fucked her. He hadn't been this vigorous in...possibly ever. "And two or three inches longer than you." He pounded. "Maybe more."

"Fuck," Evan growled as he pounded without restraint. Jackie fell herself rising with pleasure.

"Mm, Baby, you should see him."

"Yeah, I..." Evan looked slightly embarrassed and averted his eyes, but pushed in her a little harder anyway. "Tell me how he fucked you."

Her heart skipped a beat. "So hard. And fast. In control."

She remembered how Grant used to toss her around, and put her hands on Evan's ribs until, confused, he stopped pumping and backed out. Jackie smiled at him with a wicked gleam in her eyes, and rolled over onto her stomach beneath him. She raised her ass in the air and looked over her shoulder.

"Like this," she said, waggling for him. "He used to like to fuck me like this." She felt Evan steady his tip and slide himself fully inside.

"Oh, yeah, just like that." She moaned, stretching herself into cat pose. "Except deeper." She heard Evan grunt, and his fingers clamped harder into her hips. "I could barely fit him. God, I miss feeling so full." His thighs slapped against her as he fucked her harder than ever, and she buried her face into the mattress with a low, joyful laugh.

"You like hearing about his big cock, Baby? How he used to stretch me and make me come?"

"Oh, yeah," Evan immediately agreed, his thrusts becoming punctuated and sure.

"You wanna see it, don't you?"

"Yes."

"You want to see Grant's big, hard, veiny cock?"

"Oh, yes."

"Pushing inside me…"

"Oh, god."

"…fucking me…"

"Yes."

"…pounding me till I come…"

"Oh, fu…yes!"

"…emptying himself inside me…"

Evan's feral cry and desperate grip on her hips, along with vivid thoughts of Grant, pushed Jackie shuddering and squealing over the edge.

After a few final thrusts, her husband pulled out, and flopped down beside her in the bed. She rolled over into him, feeling his fluid leak onto her thighs.

Satisfied and sleepy, she would have loved to doze off in Evan's arms, but knew she at least had to get up first to pee.

A familiar smell but her nose as she entered the hall, and her pulse immediately jumped into her throat. As she crossed the hall to go into the bathroom, she looked over to Grant's bedroom. The door was closed.

Fuck.

How long has he been home?

My god. What did he hear?

12

Evan pulled himself gently out of bed so as to not wake his wife, and pulled on the sweatpants he earlier discarded on the floor. He looked back at Jackie with nerves bubbling up in his stomach. How much of what they said last night would she remember? How much did he hope she did?

He told his semi-hard cock not to harden as he replayed the night while using the bathroom.

Did I really agree I wanted to see her ex-boyfriend fuck her?

He looked in the mirror as he washed his hands.

Yup.

Do I even actually want that?

He blushed, even though he was alone, and dried off his hands with a towel.

Yup.

He padded out into the kitchen, and jarred to a stop upon seeing Grant.

Shirtless again.

Goddamn.

He felt a stir as he looked at his pecs.

"Hey," Evan said, lifting his hand in a wave. "G'morning."

Grant held a big bowl in the crook of his arm, beating a bunch of eggs with a whisk. He paused and tipped his chin up with a smile.

"Morning! How was your Thanksgiving?"

"Uh, good," Evan said, thoughts filling again with the night before. "Very good." He couldn't keep his eyes from falling to the front of Grant's grey sweats, remembering Jackie's formidable description the night before. The obviously unsecured bulge made Evan's face burn, and he watched as it swayed with the motion of Grant's vigorous whisk.

"How was yours?" He asked, leaning on the island bar facing Grant. The shower turned on down the hall.

Jackie must be awake.

"It was good," Jake answered, pouring his egg mixture into a dish filled with cut up meat and veggies. "Low key. I think today might be even better." He topped the mixture with cheese. "For one, I love leftovers; turkey frittata is gonna be good. And more importantly," he moved to wash his hands in the sink, "I think I'll be fucking your wife."

Evan's jaw fell open and Grant just looked annoyingly amused. "What?" He sputtered, taken aback. Grant smiled and dried his hands.

"I heard you last night." He shrugged, and Evan's heart dropped down to his balls.

"What?"

Grant chuckled and crossed his arms, leaning confidently back against next to the stove.

"I heard you. Fucking your wife. While she was practically begging for it to be me." The veins and bulges of his body worked together to force Evan's eyes to his crotch. "Well." He looked smug. "You were both begging for it to be me."

Evan didn't know what to say. "I mean, that was just talk."

Grant squinted at him skeptically, a condescending smile shaping his handsome face. "Was it?"

Evan opened his mouth, but nothing came out. He helplessly held his palms up, unable to answer.

The shower turned off, and Grant smirked and moved his frittata to the oven. He set the timer for fifteen minutes and swaggered over to stand at Evan's back.

A chill ran down his spine as the man's energy hovered only inches behind.

"Take off your shirt, Evan."

Evan swallowed hard. He desperately wanted to obey.

Grant's voice rumbled closely over the tiny hairs on his ears, sending goosebumps all over his skin. "Take off your shirt."

Evan pulled his shirt up over his head and set it down on the counter. His nipples poked into the air.

"Uh oh. You're in it now." Evan could hear the comfortable teasing in the larger man's voice. A finger ran down his spine. "Pants."

Unthinking, heart thumping, Evan pushed his pants quickly down to his feet. His cock sprung up hard, tapping the underside of the counter. He was ashamed, but more than anything, exhilarated.

Grant clapped his hand on the back of his neck and gave it a squeeze. "Good boy."

Evan knew he couldn't be more than a few months younger, but, still. He didn't mind.

In fact, he kind of hoped he heard it again.

"That was so fucking easy," Grant laughed, coming around Evan's side and folding his arms as he leaned against the counter and looked down at Evan's erect cock.

Grant moved his hand down his own abs and between his tight, cut gutters, confidently commanding Evan's eyes. His long, hard rod stood up and out in his sweats, and suddenly, Evan's mouth was intensely dry. He licked his lips.

Grinning, Grant hooked his thumbs under the waistband of his pants.

"Think of how easy it'll be with your wife." He lifted and pulled at his pants, revealing a thick, bulging, porn-worthy cock.

Grant reached for Evan, putting his hand flat under his cock, lifting it, but giving none of the stimulation he desperately craved. Grant held his own cock out straight as if to compare. Humiliation tickled his balls.

"Oh," Evan whispered, feeling a jolt when he finally looked up from Grant's cock and into his eyes.

Yes.

Grant looked down to his mouth and smiled. For some reason, he thought the taller man would lean down and capture his mouth, and instinctively, he parted his lips.

"Frittata will be ready in about ten minutes," Grant said, tilting his strong chin up with self-satisfaction. He pulled his sweats back up by didn't bother to try to hide the tent.

"Take it out. Then, if you want, come and join." He looked down at Evan's cock with a smirk and backed up, heading out to the hall. Delighted with power, he pointed at Evan. "Don't move a muscle till then. Just stand there, and listen, and think about what I'm doing with your wife." He grinned. "And what she's doing for me."

Grant stretched as he turned into the hall and Evan swallowed at the strength in his back. As soon as the man turned out of sight, Evan turned his attention to the oven timer.

Nine minutes and forty-three seconds to go.

13

"Oh, my god, Grant!" Jackie stopped the towel from drying her hair and pulled it close to her naked chest. "Sorry, I just assumed it was Evan!"

She had just said "Come in" to the knock on the door without really giving it much thought. Taking in his hard, broad chest, and the obvious steel tenting his sweats, she mused that she didn't regret the mistake.

She shifted her stance as she looked at his body, feeling the slickness increasing between her folds. She let her towel sway to the side.

His smoldering eyes raked over the now-revealed side of her breast.

"Nah, Evan's out in the kitchen," he said, then looked into her eyes with a smirk. "We had a good talk."

Jackie's throat went suddenly dry, and she pulled her bottom lip in between her teeth. "Oh?" The terrycloth fibers brushed over her nipple.

"Mm," Grant raised his eyebrows and nodded confirmation, cocky smugness taking over his face. "Told him I heard you last night."

He took a step toward her, folding his arms, causing his already hard muscles to flex. She warmed as he drew closer, feeling bashful but still holding his eyes.

"That I know how bad you want me to fuck you." He moved forward another step, his magnetism increasing at he neared.

"How bad he wants me to fuck you." He cocked his head with a smirk and hooked his thumbs under his waistband. He pulled and jiggled, and she flushed at the way it swung his covered rod around. She wanted him to just take it out. She struggled to lift her eyes back up to his, and when she did, he took another step forward, completely invading her space. Slowly, just a few inches, she lowered her towel.

"He's out there, naked," he said, and Jackie felt the heat of his eyes on her skin. "Poor guy is hard as a rock."

Jackie's pulse pounded hard in her throat. She held his eyes and set her towel down on the dresser. She dripped as he looked at her. He always did like her tits.

"Your husband's coming in here in, like, five minutes," he said, brushing her nipple with the back of his finger. The gentle toucg tore through her like lightning, and she felt dizzy as he pulled his hand away. "He practically begged to walk in on a show."

Without hesitation, Jackie reached between them and wrapped her hand around Grant's hard, clothed cock. With a groan, he leaned down and covered her lips with his own, and with that, Jackie's inhibitions burst open.

She opened her mouth to let his tongue claim hers, hastily pulling him closer by his cock. She melted into his powerful arms as they enveloped her, and greedily reached into his pants.

"Oh, god!" She called out, her lower lip being pulled between his. She had assumed she'd remembered a glorified version of him, but, no. His manhood was even thicker than she'd recalled.

One broad hand at the small of her back, he moved the other to push up and squeeze her breast.

"Yes,"Jackie whispered, as he rolled her pert nipple under his thumb.

"Louder," he said, smiling, and bent to take her earlobe into her mouth. "Your husband is listening."

He pinched her nipple and she gasped out an "Oh!", pulling his cock up out of his pants. "Oh!" This one was a yell.

"Grant, god!" Her voice was a mixture of lust, desperation, and plea, and Grant grunted a hard, low, mumble in response. She let go on his shaft to wrap her arms around him, gripping, grasping, pulling herself so close as he kissed her, she felt the large vein of his cock on her stomach.

In the distance, a high pitched sound went off, but she was too wrapped up in Grant to care. Ever since she saw him again - or maybe even before - she had been craving the hot, commanding press of his skin.

His hand pushed down to cover a cheek of her ass, and he circled before giving a squeeze.

Slap!

His palm cracked down on her rear, and she squealed, thrusting her hands up the back of his neck into his hair.

She leaned back from his mouth, panting, which only pressed his member harder against her body. He was starving.

"You remember how I like it," she said, smiling into his eyes as a dark, wicked gleam sharpened his. He thrust her back onto the bed and she shrieked, slick excitement running hot down her thigh.

"Hm," he smirked, and pulled off his sweats. "Just wait."

Her insides fluttered as she watched up from the bed, enjoying the view of his hulking body as he eyed her like prey and strutted to the bed.

He grabbed her hips, rough and hard, and moaned in anticipation as he dropped to his knees.

Rough, impatient hands dragged down her thighs and onto her knees, pushing her legs apart.

"Ohhh, yes. Yes, yes!" She groaned out as his lips claimed her thigh, and her hands raised to her breasts as if out of their own accord.

Grant licked and nipped his way up the inside of her wet thigh as his hands explored the curves of her body.

"Grant! Fuck!"

"Mm, not yet," he teased, circling the tip of his finger just barely between her folds before returning both hands to hold down her hips. God, she loved the way he took control of her body.

In a smooth, quick motion, Grant stood and hoisted her body, tossing her squarely in the center of the bed.

Out of the corner of her eye, she saw some motion, and guilt waved over her as she remembered: *Evan!*

She turned her head to find that the motion was her husband standing, stroking himself, bright, wild pleasure like embers in his eyes. He was staring at her like she was the most magical thing, and licked his lips as his gaze quickly shifted to Grant. He looked back to Jackie, excitement heaving his chest, and gave her an overwhelmed little nod.

Jackie closed her eyes, trying to take it all in, but popped them open as Grant's wide, heavy hands pressed down the mattress on either side of her head.

She was lost in him again. "Oh, god."

Grant hovered over her, looking in her eyes as he lowered himself to his forearms, bringing his face within inches of hers. His long, turgid cock pressed down flat on the top of her stomach between them, and he slipped one of his hands into her hair.

Panting, slow motion, her wet pussy beating with the thunderous booms of her heart, she shuddered at the connection she found in his eyes. It scared her - it moved her - and she couldn't look away.

Tenderly, her fingertips trailed up the backs of his hard, defined arms, till they get came to rest on his back. With the new cleaned, her breasts pushed up firmly into his broad chest, and she felt the pressure of him deep inside.

Breaking their eye contact to lean down to her neck, Grant opened his mouth greedily on her throat.

"Mm," she moaned, starting to rock her hips, and felt the vibration of her voice on his lips. She couldn't ignore the protruding rock poking out hard between them.

Nipping under her jaw, and finally meeting her lips in a passionate kiss, Grant pushed his hands onto her ribs and up, up, up, grazing her nipples and lifting under her arms, the motion swinging her hands from his shoulders up to the mattress above her head.

Tongue sliding and gliding in a dance with her own, Grant continued to drive his hands up, until he pressed her wrists into the bed.

God, yes!

She deepened the kiss.

"I'm not going to fuck you," he said, and it buzzed like a saw near her head.

"What?" She said, nearly panicked, as she writhed, dripping, under his solid form. She heard heightened breathing and the rhythmic fap of her husband standing beside them, and she searched Grant's arrogant eyes.

"I mean, I am," he said, grinding his hips against her. He smiled. "Just not yet. Not now." He transferred both her wrists to the control of one hand, and sent the other in a gruff, sliding journey over her skin. His lips brushed hot against her ear.

"I need to taste you," he whispered, and the tip of his finger teased her soaked opening. She felt him smile against her skin. "And I know you want my cock in your mouth."

Jackie gasped, turning her head in excited pleasure, and sank her teeth into his forearm with a smile.

"Ah, I forgot about that," he growled in delight, and lifted himself from on top of her. His cock sprung up as he rolled onto his back, and with everything in her, Jackie wanted to climb on top of him and let her hot, slick cunt stretch around him.

Instead, she rolled over, made quick, bold eye contact with Evan, and then waggled her ass up in the air toward him. She crawled toward Grant, eyes fixed on his bulging, thick cock. She practically drooled.

Fucking finally.

14

Jackie's ass flaunted up in front of him as Evan stroked his rigid, tingling dick, his mouth dangling open in awe.

Holy fuck, he thought to himself, or maybe even whispered aloud. Who could know? He was completely outside of his body.

Pink and swollen, Jackie's pussy glistened just out of his reach. He wanted her. But somehow, he wanted to stand there and watch even more.

At least for the moment, anyway.

Leaning around on one foot, Evan could see his wife wrap her hand around Grant's cock. He had looked thick on his own, but in her hand, even thicker. Her fingertips didn't even touch her thumb. He squeezed himself as he watched. His fingers easily overlapped.

With a moan, she lowered her lips down around Grant's wide mushroom head. A vice of envy and jealousy clamped Evan's balls. He really wanted to be both of them.

Jackie lowered herself onto his cock, getting about half of him in her mouth before gagging and pulling herself off. She moaned and swung her leg up and over Grant's head, squaring her knees on either side of his head.

Grant's hands roughly caressed the swell of her ass, gripping, grasping, and kneading. As she licked around the tip of his cock, he pulled her down against his mouth.

"Oh, god!" Jackie yelled, thrusting her mouth down on him again, as he buried his mouth in her folds.

Evan's cock was leaking; he was dying to come, but he was afraid if he did, the fantasy might break. He was scared to think of when reality might crash over him - for now, he would much rather stay deliriously horny and hard.

Jackie worked to take in more of Grant's girth as she wildly moaned and slid against her ex's face.

"Oh, god," she whimpered, stroking him as she leaned down to suck on his balls. "I want your cock inside me," she begged, licking up his shaft and sliding her lips over his head again.

"It is," he laughed, and put his tongue back over her clit.

"No," she said desperately, but continued to keep proving his point. "I want you *inside* me," she said, and Evan chilled at the sound of her voice. "That big, strong cock slamming into my pussy," she said, and shrieked as Grant teasingly slapped her ass, and grunted with his tongue inside her.

"I miss your cock. The way you fucked me."

She slurped, and Evan stroked himself harder.

"Deep places no one but you can reach."

He felt slighted, but it only clenched his balls more.

Grant slapped her ass again and she shrieked, but the sound was muffled by his cock in her mouth.

"Oh, Grant."

Evan panted as he watched the pair buck.

"Grant!'

The other man's name filled him with the sharp, burning pressure of desire.

Grant squeezed and slapped Jackie's ass again, and Evan noticed her face was the picture of lust.

As she rode the man's face, her moans grew higher and higher, and she began jerking him hard toward her wide open mouth.

15

"You look relaxed." Jill's tone was friendly but her eyes accusatory, as she pulled a bag of popcorn from the microwave and poured it into a bowl.

Jackie pulled open a bag of M&Ms and poured them into the bowl with a smile.

"I got good sleep." She shrugged. "Took a bath."

She blushed as she still felt the fullness of Grant's cock as if he were still inside her mouth.

"Uh huh," said Jill, rolling her eyes, and set the microwave to pop another bag. "Well, whatever you're doing, keep it up. You're, like, beaming." She smiled at her sister. "It's cute."

Jackie had flopped, exhausted, onto her back after Grant had brought her to climax twice with his mouth, and finally, with a deafening roar, had emptied himself onto her tongue.

He had rested his hand on her thigh as she'd struggled to steady her breath, and gave her a gentle squeeze before lifting himself from the bed.

Evan had stopped stroking himself, though, as evidenced by his protruding, turgid cock, he hadn't yet reached orgasm himself. Wide-eyed, he stared at Grant as the larger man had walked up, way too much in his space, and put his wide, worked hand on Evan's face. Grant had looked down at Evan, obviously surveying his cock, and looked back into his eyes with a smile. He said something to Evan, but Jackie couldn't hear what, and then playfully patted his cheek.

Evan nodded and Grant turned to walk away; both husband and wife watched him go. Evan came to cuddle behind Jackie's spent body in the bed, but just moments later, the musical alarm had gone off on her phone: time to get ready for leftovers and a movie at her mom and dad's.

Now, the sisters walked into the living room and distributed popcorn, and Jackie turned off the lights. It was early in the day and her parents' curtains weren't blackout, so it didn't do much to set a theater mood. It didn't matter. Everyone was eager to play along with the fun.

Jackie sat across her husband's lap in her favorite big chair, and was delighted to find him a little bit hard under her leg. She tried to keep any reaction off her face, but knew he noticed her notice by the gentle blush that crept up his face. She wiggled her eyebrows while offering him popcorn.

The movie they watched couldn't hold her attention, but Jackie wasn't sure if it was because it was actually boring, or if she was just too caught up in memories of the morning to focus.

Her phone buzzed in her lap.

A text from Grant: *"Been wanting to do that for awhile."*

She felt her husband's eyes observe.

"Me too," she responded.

"Already wanting to do it again."

She looked up at her family squished together on the couch. They were all so immersed in the movie. *"Me too."* She responded again.

Evan's hand moved slightly in her thigh by her knee, but when she looked at him, he seemed to be just watching the movie, too.

"And more." Read the next text, and Jackie couldn't help but squirm. The motion caused Evan's hand to slide just slightly higher up her jeans. She erased different starts to her next text three times before she found what she wanted to say.

"*Show me.*" She added an eggplant symbol, then quickly clicked off her screen and put her phone face-down in her lap, cheeks burning. Evan squeezed her knee.

Her phone buzzed and, heart fluttering, Jackie looked around suspiciously to find her whole family still safely looking away. She swiped and then heated as a picture of Grant's thick, proud dick filled up her screen.

"*Already hard again. Can't stop thinking about fucking you.*"

She perceived Evan's eyes scorching into her skin. She loved feeling so ellicit.

"*It's been a long time since I've had anything close to that big.*" She felt her husband's already chubbed cock harden a little beneath her. "*I'm not sure I'll still be able to fit you.*" Evan's thumb rubbed on her thigh, and his legs shifted a little beneath her.

"*Something tells me you're still going to try…*"

Jackie smiled. Evan stiffened beneath her.

"*Yes. Fuck me. Tonight.*"

Her heartbeat drowned out the sound of the movie. She couldn't wait for the credits to roll. She was desperate to get back to Grant.

"What about your cute little husband?" The next text said.

Before she did reply, Evan reached for her phone, and gently took it from her hands. He wrote something quickly, set it back in her lap, and went back to watching the movie.

She swiped it open.

"Well, you can try to fuck him, too."

16

Though they had only been at Jackie's parents for a few hours, it was already dark and crisp by the time Evan and Jackie got home. Well, to Grant's house - but weirdly, it did feel somehow like home.

Nerves swarmed inside him as they let themselves in, but Grant was nowhere to be found. They took off their coats, and Evan caught a warm glow from the gazebo outside.

"I think he's outside," he announced, his excitement a low, thumping hum. Jackie joined him to look out the window.

"Probably smoking," she said, and looked up to Evan while hugging his arm. "Do you wanna...go...join him?" The hope and thrill in her eyes mirrored exactly the way he felt.

He nodded, swallowing to counteract his suddenly dry throat. "Yeah." He headed out toward the back door, but Jackie pulled on his hand, and yanked him back toward her to give him a kiss. She deepened it, putting both her hands on his face, and while it boosted excitement, it also helped calm his nerves.

She pulled back, just barely, and looked up into his eyes. "Are you ready?" She was earnest, and it melted his heart. Her sincerity made him stop and consider it.

Picturing the things they were both about to do, Evan leaned down to kiss her and then gave her a grin. He took a small step forward so the bulge in his pants poked insistently into her hip.

"So ready."

Grant lounged under a blanket on cushions he'd moved from his patio onto his gazebo floor, and took a long, drawn-out puff from his blunt. He looked into the glow of a little electric fireplace he had set up inside, it's cinnamon warmth highlighting the sharp, manly lines of his face.

The man exhaled through a smile when he saw them, and propped himself up on his elbow. As the blanket shifted, Evan realized he was naked.

"Take off your clothes and join me," Grant said, gesturing to the cozy nest of comfort around him.

Evan looked to the trees surrounding them, trying to gauge just how private Grant's yard and the gazebo were. By the time he looked back, Jackie had already stripped off her shirt, and was busy removing her pants.

Yup. Okay. Doing this. Nerves broiled his body, and suddenly, he couldn't get his clothes off quickly enough.

Jackie's breasts jiggled as she flounced across the gazebo over to Grant, making "brr" noises as she went. He lifted his blanket, and with a grin toward his crotch, lowered her body right next to his.

"Whew!" Grant laughed, putting his arm around Jackie and making a face as if he were holding ice. "Better warm you up."

Jealousy burned in Evan as he watched his wife breathe smoke into her ex's close, open mouth, and finally, he remembered the plan this time was actually to join them.

There was nontoom under the blanket next to Jackie, so instead, he sat next to Grant. As he descended, Grant turned and eyed him appreciatively, putting a hand on his back as he sat.

Grant's touch set Evan's skin on fire, and he felt dizzy as the man leaned in and blew smoke between his lips.

He wanted more.

Grant turned back to Jackie and Evan watched as the two touched tongues. His wife gave Grant a small, sly smile, and suddenly, the blanket over his crotch moved rhythmically up and down.

The larger, broader man gave a soft gentle chuckle, and slowly, swiveled his attention back to Evan.

"God, she can't keep her hands off my cock. Never could." Jackie moaned in agreement, hand still moving under the blanket as she leaned forward for the blunt Grant held in reach of her lips. "You ever touch another man, Evan?"

Evan's eyebrows rose and his neck prickled in chills. Grant held up the blunt and Evan leaned forward, looking the man in the eyes as he put his lips to it and inhaled.

"No," he said, enjoying the way Grant watched the smoke spill from his mouth. He tried to be brave. "Not yet."

Grant smiled, took a puff, and passed the blunt off to Jackie. He leaned close and confidently into Evan's space. Slowly, steadily, he blew a stream at Evan's mouth, and Evan couldn't help but lean in himself to take in what Grant gave.

Grant finished exhaling but didn't move back, and simply smirked at Evan's face, just a breath away. Evan looked to his lips and then into his eyes, seeing Jackie In his periphery, mesmerized and still stroking. Evan looked to Grant's lips again.

Evan would never quite know for sure if he closed the space between them, or if Grant had leaned into him first. Either way, their lips met in a ravenous battle of power, lust, and control. With his wife still stroking the bigger man's cock, it was clear Evan was not the winner. The funny thing was, he didn't have any desire to be.

Grant's tongue prodded between Evan's lips, and he let out a heavy moan. He ached to be pulled close, handled, and used. He whimpered as Grant pulled briefly away, but his stomach flipped to see him lift up the blanket, giving Jackie a grin.

A wicked smile split Jackie's face, and she disappeared down below the blanket. Pleasure took over the handsome man's face as Jackie replaced her hand with her head.

"Oh, yes," the man muttered, and Evan's wife groaned. Without any warning, Grant's hand slid over Evan's thigh and immediately held his hard dick.

Evan yelped in bliss and couldn't help it - he lunged himself into Grant's mouth.

Grant stroked twice as he chuckled, his lips still pressed against Evan's, and Evan thought he might come then and there. Grant kept backing his lips taunting just out of reach, using denial and little spurts of reward as an almost immediate means to subdue him.

Body burning with arousal, Evan trembled desperately just out of reach of Grant's mouth. Jackie pulled the blanket back off her head; apparently, they were all heating.

Jackie slurped off Grant's cock with a gasp and a moan, and stroked a few times before returning. Evan could cry out with envy.

"You want to taste too, don't you?" Feathers of Grant's breath caressed over his lips, and he gasped as the man gently squeezed his shaft.

"Yes," he whispered, and Grant flicked his tongue on Evan's lower lip with a grin.

Electricity pulsed through Evan as he watched desire and power flare in Grant's eyes. "So go ahead."

Evan looked down to Jackie licking down the side of Grant's shaft, as she looked up at her husband eyelids drooping heavily with lust.

"Mmm," she moaned in welcome. "Come suck him with me, Baby. I don't have much longer to I'm going to have to beg him to fuck me."

Nerves rolled inside Evan's stomach again, and his skin blushed from forehead to feet.

He could only stare in wonder as Grant confidently sat back, stretching his arms out on the cushions life some carefree, entitled king. Though he could feel the magnetic pull of Grant's body, his inner voice held him back.

You can't really want that, he thought, staring hard and naked at his wife on Grant's dick.

I do, the other part of him fought back.

But you're straight.

He licked his lips, gravity pulling him down just a tiny bit down.

Ok, but I want him.

Jackie looked at him, shining with mischief, and moaned as she popped off Grant's head. Without another thought, Evan slid to his knees, and put his lips on the other man's cock.

Immediately, Jackie groaned, excitement and approval clear in her voice, and it only encouraged him more. He pulled the thick tip into his mouth.

"Mm!" His mind and spirit expanded from the pressure poking into his palate, and suddenly, urgently, he could not get enough. He wrapped his hand around Grant's base, and tried to take more of him in. He gagged, and Grant pulled him up and off by his hair. The larger man laughed.

"Easy," he soothed, his tone betraying the tight tug hair, which tilted Evan's head back and forced him to look in his eyes. "We've got time." He positioned his lips at his cock again. "Besides, your wife is the best. She'll teach you. Just put your hand around me."

Evan wrapped his hand around Grant, and Jackie leaned forward and kissed Evan's neck. It was the burn of hot liquor straight to his veins, and he closed his eyes as she kissed him again. In his own arousal, his hand twitched around Grant.

This feels good.

Jackie kissed up to Evan's lips, and, nerves calmed by the familiarity, he lost himself in the kiss. His hand moved up and down Grant in soft, short strokes, as easily as if he were touching himself. Grant hissed, and he and Jackie's tongues tangled together in bliss.

The more heated their kiss got, the faster Evan stroked, and the lower they got down near Grant. Eyes closed, immersed in his dreamlike euphoria, Evan was not expecting the gentle prodding at the sides of their mouths.

As they broke a bit from a kiss only to lean back in for another, the head of Grant's cock slipped between their tongues.

"Mm!" Evan moaned out again. Their lips suctioned around the solid tip, and made a smacking sound when Grant pulled back out.

Husband and wife continued kissing as Grant continued to slide between, gently guiding the backs of their heads and intermittently hissing his pleasure.

One of the times their kiss broke apart, Jackie turned and slid Grant's cock into her mouth, keeping her eyes glued to Evan as she did. She came off and held it out for Evan to try, and easily, he took him inside.

Switching off, taking their time, sucking deeper and deeper, Evan and Jackie shared her ex's big cock. Eyes closed as Evan sucked, he realized Jackie was no longer down next to him, but had pulled up to sit at Grant's side.

The man had his powerful arm around her back and commandingly kissed her lips, their hands needfully exploring each other's bodies. Grant cupped her breast and she whimpered as he tweaked her nipple between his finger and thumb.

Evan had taken Grant deeper and deeper, until the tip pushed at the back of his throat. He loved it.

"Fuck me," Jackie whispered breathlessly, her hands on Grant's face, and pushed herself up onto her knees before lifting one and sweeping it over his legs.

Evan moaned around Grant's rod, a fresh wave of arousal pumping through him at the sight of his wife's beautiful ass.

"Fuck me!" She was louder - begging. Without thinking, he let Grant's thick cock slip out of his mouth, and held it steady right under his wife.

"Yes. Yes, yes!" Jackie pleaded, as Grant's hands came around to grip hard on her ass. "Please." His bulging purple head disappeared between her folds and she wheezed as she inhaled.

"Yes! Please!"

17

Even just the tip of Grant's cock stretched Jackie in a way she'd been missing for years. Closing her eyes, she rested her hands against his shoulder and clavicle, bracing as she lowered herself down.

"Yes, Grant," she panted, so wet she dripped down his shaft. "More." She lowered herself down further, but paused to adjust to the fullness. She opened her eyes again, and her stomach flipped at the way Grant looked at her. She slipped down another inch.

"God, you feel good," he rasped, his low voice full of gravel. Both of his hands slid firmly up her back in support, and she leaned forward to give him a kiss.

Eliciting gasps from both of them, he slipped in another good bit.

"Oh, god!" Jackie cried, pulling away from his lips, but then attacking again with a vigor. His tongue explored hers, a mix of starving and savoring, and she brought her hands to either side of his face. He looked her in the eyes and started slowly, rhythmically, rocking his hips, pulling out, and then only back as far as she'd had him.

Mouth falling open in total euphoria, Jackie slid her hands to the back of his neck and into his hair. She leaned forward again and slipped her tongue between her lips, and slowly started rocking around him. As their lips wrestled together, a mixture of familiarity and need, and she gradually worked herself down on his dick.

"You're so fucking thick, Grant," she said, breathless, head leaned back as Grant bit and kissed down her neck. "You're so much bigger than my husband." She thought Evan would like it, but it felt naughty to say, and gave her even more of a rush.

She quickened her rocking around him arching back further as her ex made his way to her tits. Be took a nipple between his wet lips, and she called out into the crisp night.

She lowered fully onto his cock and he looked up into her eyes. His intensity fluttered her heart, and her walls gave a quick *thump* around him. Slowly, she resumed grinding her hips.

"I love being inside you," he gruffed earnestly, still looking her right in the eye. She bounced a little harder.

"I love taking your cock." For a moment, things between them felt almost too intimate - almost too good to be true. In a rush of adrenaline, she kissed him again. And rocked…

…bucked…

…*slammed* her hips, feverishly up and down on his cock.

"Oh, god!" She cried, banging down hard on his lap as she dug her nails into his skin. He was so thick and filling, each reentry felt like it might burst her apart.

"Right there," she whispered, the plea almost drowned out by the slaps of their skin. The angle at which he pulled almost-out each time rubbed his cock roughly against her clit. "Just like that. Oh, yes!"

She couldn't stop the string of approving curses and swears from spilling out between her lips.

"More. Harder. Fuck yes, Grant, give me that big fucking cock."

He held her hips tight as he pumped harder inside her, a look of bliss consuming his face. Each thrust shot her higher up before she came crashing back down, and arousal was starting to overwhelm her.

"Yes. Yes…"

The clapping of skin, the low groans of pleasure…

"Yes…"

The searing, deep force of his cock…

"Yes!"

Over, and over, and over…

"Grant!"

The cry started out as a shriek but turned into a squeak as the man continued fucking her through her orgasm.

She dug her fingernails into his chest as he slowed, but didn't lessen, his thrusts. Jackie was no way unhappy with her sex life with Grant but - *dear god!* - it had been years since she came quite like…

"Oh, oh god!" She panted. Just at the point she had been about to fall over, exhausted, Grant caught some magic angle again. Now avoiding her clit altogether, just thrusting and pumping himself deep, deep inside, Grant had pushed her onto a second wave.

Slower than the first, steady like a deep, heavy bass drum, the pressure inside get built up into a point, sharpening, deepening, threatening to pop her and let her release.

Jackie rolled her head back, giving up all control of her body, and smiled as he ex slammed inside. Still able to read her, he slowed himself down to a few final, punctuated thrusts, and she leaned down to kiss him as he pushed her right over the edge.

Tongues languid together as she came clenching around him, they held each other as they panted in pleasure. Jackie laughed as she pulled herself up off his still very hard, slick sticky dick.

She flopped onto the cushions and watched him, completely spent, but so lustful. She may have been too exhausted to take him anymore, but as she looked at him - all rough, manly determination as he stood from his seat - Jackie couldn't quiet her thoughts.

I need this man to fuck me again.

He stood, eyes trained on her wide-eyed, self-stroking husband, and his wet cock bobbed up into the air.

And again, and again, and again.

18

Evan looked up at Grant in awe as he rose, and a fresh wave of adrenaline overtook him. He let go of his smaller, hard, leaking cock as the big man quietly entered his space.

The hairs stood on Evan's neck, each heartbeat like a battery being placed on his tongue. He felt almost threatened, but he welcomed the threat.

Please, please, please.

He couldn't say the words out loud.

Grant's long, turgid cock pointed right at his lips, and he parted them, but Grant stayed still. They stared into each other's eyes, and Grant reached forward to touch Evan's face.

Evan shuddered. It wasn't so much just attraction, but the feel of being under his control.

Grant smirked, his eyes lighting, and he gripped more firmly around Evan's chin. With a grunt, he pushed Evan back off his balance.

Stumbling, heart racing, Evan dropped onto his back, and Grant got down and approached him like some large, wild cat. His hand came down rough on Evan's shoulder, and hoisted him onto his side.

"Roll over," Grant said, landing a slap on Evan's ass, and Evan surprised even himself with his excited, high whimper. He had never been handled like this before, and he felt the joy of it low in his guts. In a scurry, he rolled onto his forearms and knees.

"Good boy," Grant said, and the words washed over him, warm and reassuring, but scattered as the larger man wrapped himself around Evan's back.

"Oh god," Evan whispered, ending in a low, heavy *hmph* as Grant's weight dropped him down to the floor. Dense muscle, hot skin, his big, hard, strong, dominant body - Evan opened his mouth against the blanket in euphoric submission. He had never been touched like that before.

The man held his forearms down, pinned out in front of his head, and he lowered himself into Evan's back.

"I've missed fucking your wife, Man," he said gruffly, his shaft resting along the space between his cheeks. "And, mm, I can't wait to get my dick in you."

Evan groaned and balled his hands into the blanket beneath him, mouth open and slightly smiling against the warm woolen blanket.

Wow...

He wanted to be used.

Grant's cock slid down his crack, the head of it poking his thigh, then the large man shifted his weight into his arms, which pinned Evan, and lifted his hips to get his rod back in place.

Savoring the pressure and control of Grant's body, Evan found himself raising his hips up as well. He wanted more and more of him.

"You liked watching me fuck your wife?" Grant rumbled, pushing practically all of his weight onto Evan's whole body.

"Yes," Evan whispered, feeling small and pleased to be under the bigger man's control.

"Liked watching my big, hard cock slip inside her?"

"Fuck yes," Evan immediately answered, and Grant slid himself roughly between the curves of his ass again.

"Pushing so much deeper inside you than you've ever been?"

"Yes," he hissed out, and then gasped as Grant's head began poking between his cheeks. "Yes."

Evan though Grant was already using brute strength to hold the smaller man down, he made a shoving motion, pushing some of the air out of him. Evan wanted to laugh at the pleasure of being so overwhelmed.

Grant's cock tapped against Evan's hole.

"You want me, don't you?"

"Yes." It was a breath; Evan didn't have to think.

"Yes, what?"

"Yes, please!"

Grant laughed, and leaned forward, putting pressure against him. He felt dizzy, almost out of his mind.

"Please, *what?*" Grant said, clearly taunting and amused.

"Fuck me," Evan answered, arching his ass toward the man. He felt like he'd die if the larger man didn't, and like he might live forever if only he would. "Fuck me. Please fuck me!"

Just the very tip of Grant pushed inside Evan, and a yelp of euphoric excitement escaped from his lungs. He'd never had anything inside him before, and the pressure felt even better than he'd hoped.

Grant's muscles flexed against him, holding him firmly, inescapably down, even though there was no way Evan would want to escape.

"Take it, Evan, take it."

Even though Evan wanted to take more - to stay under the beast of a man for hours, or maybe all night, and to feel the full, unbridled force of his cock - but the rumble of his voice and the thumping pleasure of just his tip was just too great.

"Oh fuck," he whispered, realizing the oncoming, unstoppable tide. "Fuck. Grant. Fuck!"

On the ground under Grant, surrounded and filled with his heat, Evan let go as he fell over the edge.

Body shaking, Evan's ass began clenching in rhythm, trying both to take more of and eject Grant's thick cock. His own cum spurted out under his belly, and suddenly, all he could do was breathe.

Grant pulled out from his body, with a taunting smack to his cheek, and suddenly, Jackie slithered down to the floor right beside him. Warm and comforting, she wrapped her arm around Evan, as the big, great, still-hard man stood up.

"That was the hottest fucking thing I've ever fucking seen," Jackie whispered to them both.

Grant grinned and positioned himself at their heads.

He held his swollen cock and stroked in their directions, and though Evan was exhausted - almost sleeping - he watched his wife's eyes light up. She tilted her chin and opened her mouth, and by instinct, Evan did the same.

"Tomorrow morning, I'm coming inside," Grant whispered, voice tight as his hand sailed over his dick. "You two just need to decide who."

A hot white stream of his pleasure shot out, landing on Jackie's open mouth and her tongue. Without even thinking, Evan leaned close to kiss her, as Grant's cum continued spurting out on them.

Gently, Grant put his hands on the backs of their heads, encouraging them as they kissed, and eventually, exhausted, they all laid down together in a soft, tangled knot.

19

Jackie awoke, warm, cozy, and naked in the guest room bed, to the feel of Grant's hard arms wrapped securely around her back. Slowly, she opened her eyes, and found her sleepy-faced husband looking at her with a soft smile.

"Good morning, Sexy," he whispered. "Wanna get fucked?"

Immediately, her folds became wet, and she was grateful she had gotten up just an hour before to pee. Her eyes glimmered, and instead of answering, she leaned forward to give Evan a kiss.

Soft and gentle as the morning itself, the couple's lips found and explored each other. The tenderness of her husband's hand on her ribs was contrasted by the hard, steely rod poking against her exposed backside. The dissonance was delicious, and sleepily, she wiggled her ass against her ex. She smiled into Evan's kiss as she felt the results of how much Grant enjoyed her friction.

The man's strong hands climbed sensually up her curves, and firmly gripped into her pelvis. She moaned as she deepened her husband's kiss, excited to have both their attention.

She reached down between her body and Evan's, wrapping her hand around his firm, upright cock. His tongue pressed into her mouth with insistence, and he trailed his fingers up to pinch her nipple.

She stroked Evan harder as Grant's cock began teasing her folds. Every ounce of raw desire his taunting cock pricked through her core, she channeled into kissing and touching her husband.

Both men tight around her, she tried to buck herself onto Grant's rod, but the men's bodies had her pinned up too firm. She loved the feeling of being under their power, but at the same time, she ached to be fucked.

She broke apart from her kiss with her husband but kept stroking him, looking right in his eyes.

"I need him to fuck me, Baby." She saw her words dance in his eyes. She stroked him faster. "God, I need Grant's big cock inside me again." She smiled tauntingly, remembering him the night before. "You'd understand."

She let go of him, leaving him hard and leaking, squished, pressed up to her tummy. She snaked her hand behind her and onto Grant's neck. She swivled her head to kiss the great man behind her. She hoped Evan could see their tongues collide.

"Fuck me, Grant. I want you. I need you." She could feel Evan rocking against her in front. Grant positioned his head in between her folds, then reached around to slap Evan on the ass. He smiled into their kiss, all arrogance and control. "Come inside me," she whispered, staring earnestly into his eyes.

He kissed her gently - slowly, sensuously - then backed up just enough to look in her eyes. It reminded her of when they were in love. She held her breath.

Grant's heart beat heavy and fast on her back, and chills covered the whole of her being. She melted, and at that moment, he pushed inside her, with a slow, solid, deepening stroke.

Jackie's mouth fell open as she stated at her ex, his eyes penetrating her almost as much as his cock. Unexpectedly, Evan's lips surrounded her nipple, and the electricity caused her to gasp.

Her body's growing arousal let Grant slip in a few inches more. She made a crying noise and gladly broke eye contact with Grant, letting her lips slide shut to help process the pleasure.

So full.

Deep inside me.

"Yes, Baby," she whispered, lost. He slowly backed out of her, then thrust in again. He wrapped his arms tightly around her, displacing Evan's hands on her skin. He pushed inside her again, filling her up, his rasping breath hot against the shell of her ear. This felt dangerously close to something more than just fucking.

But *god,* the fucking was good.

Grant pulled out again and she shuddered at the kids of his cock, and desperately groaned out as he spread her again.

"Oh, Grant," she said, finally opening her eyes, and her slash flipped at the hungry way he looked at her. "Grant!" He tightened his good and pushed inside her harder and faster.

"You should get on your knees, Man," Grant said through his thrusts.

Suddenly, ungracefully, but with a hard, leaking cock, Evan brought himself up to his knees.

"Good boy," Grant muttered, and leaned to kiss Jackie as he pumped inside.

Their tongues tangled together, almost sweetly at first, until lust took over, giving way to a full on brawl.

Grant spaked her with a light but cracking smack on the ass, then lifted her roughly up into her knees. He slipped out as he body wavered, but he held her hips firmly and entered again. She held him grunt and she smiled - he did always love doggy style.

"Look how much your husband likes it," Grant said, fingers tight on her hips as he increased his pistoning motions inside her. She opened her eyes. Evan leaked down his red shaft.

"Loves to watch you filled and fucked, by someone who really loves fucking you."

In her pleasure, Jackie reached forward and took Evan's cock, stroking him to match Grant's quick, potent thrusts.

"He already agreed to stay an extra day." He pumped. "That is, if you want to."

"God, yes," Jackie said, head swimming, and took her husband's cock in her mouth.

Grant continued, "And then we talk about how we go forward." He slapped her ass and she took her husband toward the back of her throat. "Cuz I can't let you go again."

Evan throbbed as he slid on her tongue, and she moaned out around his head. She surrendered her body to the slam of Grant's dick; she didn't think she could let him go either.

Pounding and slurping, with sharp shouts and moans, the trio gave themselves over to pleasure. Jackie had never been with two men at the same time, and at the moment, she felt like it was all she could ever want.

"Mm, Jax," Grant grunted, and slapped her ass, putting his hand back on her hip, holding her firm as he fucked her. "Take it, take it."

She popped off Evan's cock only long enough to speak. "Come inside me, Grant, please..."

Evan picked up right where she left off.

"Give it to her. Fuck her. Come inside my wife. Fuck, Jackie I'm gonna..." with a whimper, Evan pumped into her once more, and came with a hot spurt on her tongue. She swallowed as she licked over his head, and Grant pounded her harder and deeper inside. Evan had set off a chain reaction.

"Oh...yes...take...my...cock!" Grant's warm, hot pleasure shot out with force inside her, filling her, spilling out of her, and pushing her over the edge.

"Yes!" She called out, her pussy clamping around Grant's dick and his cum. Her entire body pulsed with the resounding beat of her heart, and as ecstacy washed over her body as heat and fulfillment, she flopped down onto the bed.

Jackie hugged her mom as Evan doled out high fives to the little ones, as they prepared to get into the car to head home.

"Don't worry," she said, moving on to hug her dad. "We'll be back for Christmas."

Evan accepted a tin foil package of leftovers from her mom - what were they supposed to do in the car with that?

"We're coming too," Jill interjected, but she held her hands out reassuringly. "But you guys can stay with Mom and Dad this time, we'll plan ahead and get a room."

"Oh, no," Jackie replied, a blush warming her face. "We already decided to stay with the same friend." Jill looked up from fixing a kid's hoodie to give her sister wide eyes. Jackie blushed and bit back a laugh as Evan lowered himself into the car. Jackie hugged her sister.

"Bitch, text me. The details are even better than you think."

I hope you enjoyed

Thanksgiving Threesome:
A Super Steamy, Romantic, Erotic MMF Bisexual Threesome Between a Loving Cuckold Husband, His Hotwife, and Her Ex

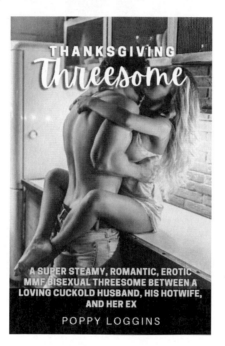

Please consider taking a moment to share your thoughts about this story.

Your review means the world to me, and helps other readers find this book!

Other books by Poppy

TATTOOED,
TAUNTED AND TEASED

An Erotic, Tawdry Tale of One
Cuckolding Couple's First Time in an
MMF Bisexual Hotwifing Threesome

POPPY LOGGINS

Even on vacation to celebrate one year of married bliss, Eve can't turn off her instinct to flirt with other men. She loves the attention and longs to be dominated, and the effect it has on her husband only adds fuel to her fire!

While getting the tattoos that drew them to town, Owen is unsettled by his intense reaction to their tattoo artist; broad, manly, and tauntingly handsome, Dom clearly is the alpha male. To Owen, it's obvious his wife wants more than these markings from his sharp, stabbing tool, and he can't really blame her. In fact, he might even want to join her...

This is a filthy, frisky erotic romp in which a fun-loving couple explores their deepest desires in a playful, dominant-led, cuckold hotwife threesome, with some bisexual contact, light humiliation, and lots and lots of lust.

Click to be taken to this book
on Amazon!

CUCKOLDING
WITH HER
KICKBOXING COACH

A Super Steamy Erotic Novella of a Hotwife
and Husband in Love, and their Lust for a
Much Stronger Man

POPPY LOGGINS

Reformed cheater and self-described slut Allie
has never been unfaithful to her husband, Ryan.
Unfortunately, that's mostly because she shut
down her libido years ago in order to be a "good
wife."

After her inner slut is awoken by a brief
flirtation with a stranger, Allie and Ryan both
get more than they bargained for when she signs
up for kickboxing class.

Under the instruction of her sexy coach, Allie
wonders if she can manage to stay loyal to her
love - and Ryan wonders why she keeps coming
home so aroused and ready for fun.

This super steamy, romantic erotica novella follows a husband and hotwife in love as they realize and explore their cuckold desires with a strong alpha male, featuring light humiliation, some MM contact, and lots of explicit sex.

Click to be taken to this book on Amazon!

HARVEST
HILL
HOTWIFE

AN EROTIC CUCKOLDING ROMP

POPPY LOGGINS

Like many young couples in love, newlyweds
Jake and Amber head to Harvest Hill for fritters,
apple picking, and their favorite seasonal, open-
air brewery. After meeting a handsome man they
had admired from a distance, the couple gets
more than they came for.

Handsome and charming (and not super
subtle), Elliot captures and commands their
attention. When Amber runs into him into the
woods, she wants to fulfill her hotwifing
fantasies. If only Jake were there to see...

This super steamy novella is a fun, light,
romantic adventure between a happy husband
and wife, with a good-natured, dominant alpha
male who makes their first cuckolding fantasy

come true. Set outdoors on a beautiful fall day, this book contains graphic depictions of semi-public sex, light consensual humiliation, and some MM bisexual contact.

Come with the couple and explore Harvest Hill!

Click to be taken to this book on Amazon!

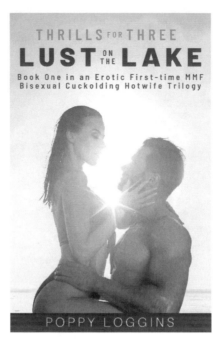

Reuniting never felt so good!

When an old college neighbor moves to town, a forgotten memory awakens hidden desires in Nicole and her husband Isaac.
Plans for a little bit of harmless flirting are set in motion when Will invites them to kick off their summer vacation at his lake house, and take on a life of their own during the boat ride there.

This novella is the first in an erotic trilogy following a loving husband and wife from their first seeds of desire for their old friend, to their first experience in a bisexual MMF cuckolding hotwife fantasy they hadn't even dared dream of.

Hop in the boat and get ready for a wet ride!

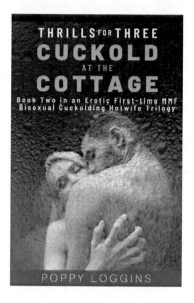

After a boat ride with an old friend turned into the romp of a lifetime, Isaac and Nicole weren't sure what to expect from the rest of their weekend holed up with him at his cottage.

Titillated to see each other in a new light, and completely enchanted by Will's raw, confident charm, the happy couple decides to let the beefy bull take control. What new things will they experience? How far will he push them? And how many times can one hotwife come??

This novella is the second in an erotic trilogy following a loving husband and wife from their first seeds of desire for their old friend, to their first experience in a bisexual MMF cuckolding hotwife fantasy they hadn't even dared dream of.

Come curl up at the cottage and enjoy the cuckolding!

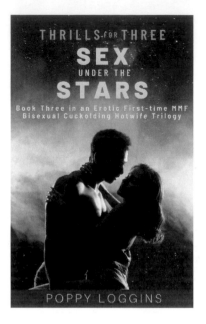

Dreams and hikes and hammocks, oh my!

After a wild start to their weekend with an old college friend, Isaac and Nicole realize their erotic desires may go deeper than either of them ever dreamed.

Join the happy couple and their weekend bull as they wake up to lust, explore their passions out under the pines, and tangle together, pushing their boundaries under the stars.

This novella is the last in an erotic trilogy following a loving husband and wife from their first seeds of desire for their old friend, to their first experience in a bisexual MMF cuckolding hotwife fantasy they hadn't even dared dream of.

Swinging in a hammock has never been more fun!

About the Author

In Poppy Loggins' world, there's really nothing sexier than a big, strong man who can dominate a couple in love.

With very few exceptions*, there is nothing Poppy loves more than writing steamy, erotic MMF cuckold romance with a focus on a happy, loving couples exploring their wildest bisexual cuckolding hotwife fantasies, and the sexy men who *rise up* to fulfill them.

Happily ever after for two, with happy endings from plenty of special guests along the way!

Visit **www.PoppyLoggins.com** for updates and extras!

*Exceptions include: sushi, hikes in the forest with her husband and dog, and doing "field research" for future stories

Made in United States
North Haven, CT
24 November 2022

27174853R00069